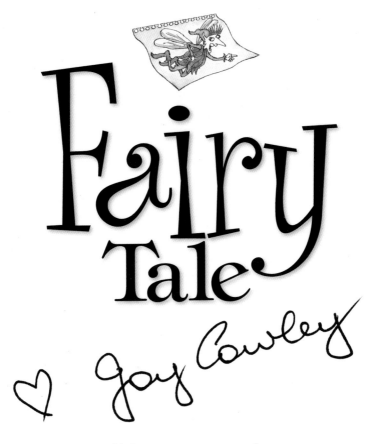

Fairy Tale

Joy Cowley

Written by Joy Cowley
Illustrated by Ian Forss

www.av2books.com

Your AV² Media Enhanced book gives you an online audio book, and a self-assessment activity. Log on to www.av2books.com and enter the unique book code from this page to access these special features.

Go to www.av2books.com, and enter this book's unique code.

BOOK CODE

G292635

AV² by Weigl brings you media enhanced books that support active learning.

AV² Audio Chapter Book Navigation

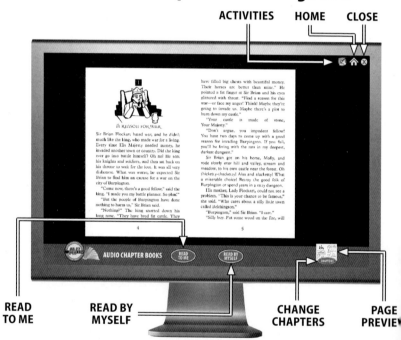

READ TO ME

READ BY MYSELF

ACTIVITIES

HOME

CLOSE

CHANGE CHAPTERS

PAGE PREVIEW

Published by AV² by Weigl
350 5th Avenue, 59th Floor
New York, NY 10118

Websites: www.av2books.com   www.weigl.com

Copyright ©2016 AV² by Weigl
All rights reserved. No part of this publication may be reproduced, stored in a retrieval system, or transmitted in any form or by any means, electronic, mechanical, photocopying, recording, or otherwise, without the prior written permission of the publisher.

First Published by Clean Slate Press.

Library of Congress Control Number: 2014949150
ISBN 978-1-4896-2519-9 (hardcover)
ISBN 978-1-4896-2520-5 (single user eBook)
ISBN 978-1-4896-2521-2 (multi-user eBook)

Printed in the United States of America in North Mankato, Minn
1 2 3 4 5 6 7 8 9 0   18 17 16 15 14
112014
WEP040914

Contents

Chapter 1	Cornflakes and Small Green Things	4
Chapter 2	The Little Lost People	9
Chapter 3	Losing the Plot	13
Chapter 4	A Brilliant Idea	16
Chapter 5	Squeals and Sour Milk	19
From the Author		23
From the Illustrator		24

Chapter 1

Cornflakes and Small Green Things

Ross Beansack, the big hairy author, sat in his writing chair, brushed some cornflakes out of his beard, and turned on his computer. This morning he wanted to write another story for children, one that would make a difference to the world. His eyebrows came together like fluffy caterpillars as he thought about the beginning. The words were there, but deep in his mind. He pushed aside thoughts of lunch and bookshops, and found what he was looking for. Yes, he had his first sentence. Quickly, he reached for the keys.

"Excuse me!" A little thing popped its little head around the side of the screen. "I said, *Excuse me!*"

The big hairy author made a funny noise and pushed his chair back. The thing was an extremely small green person with wings and eyes like shining seeds. No, it wasn't a joke someone had sent in an email. It was outside the computer, standing on his desk.

The author grabbed his beard. This is what happens when you eat cornflakes, shrimps and cheese for breakfast, he thought. He blinked hard but the tiny person didn't go away. It was no bigger than the author's first finger and it had spiky green hair.

"What are you going to write?" Its voice was shrill, worse than fingernails on a chalkboard.

The author scratched his chin and another cornflake dropped out of his beard.

"I said, *What are you going to write?*" the thing demanded.

"Like a nail scraping on concrete," said the author.

"What?"

"Oh, nothing. I was just talking to myself." The big hairy author wheeled his chair a little closer. "I'm writing a very important story. It will help children learn how to make the world a better place. I'm a published writer, you know."

"I'm aware of that." The creature put its hands on its hips. Its gauzy green wings beat rapidly. "Otherwise I wouldn't be here."

"Are you a—a fairy?" the author asked.

"Good. Your eyes work," it said. "Now, are you going to tell me what's in this important story?"

"It's about saving the rainforest and the whales." The author leaned forward. "Are you honestly, truly, a fairy?"

The little thing sighed and folded its arms over a shirt made of dark green leaves. "Have you never seen one of us before?"

The big hairy author shook his head.

"That's because we're the real endangered species. Forget about whales. Forget about trees in the rain. Fairies are nearly extinct. No publicity, you see. People don't write about us any more. Tell me, have you ever written a fairytale with fairies in it?"

The author shook his head again.

"Why not?"

The big hairy author laughed because he didn't know what else to do. "I don't write that kind of story. Fairies aren't exactly the in thing. Readers think they're old-fashioned."

"Whales are old-fashioned!" snapped the fairy. "So are big fat trees in the rainforest. What have you got against us? Huh? Aren't we big enough for a story?"

The author didn't know how to answer. He was still sure he was seeing things. Cornflakes, shrimps and cheese could be giving his eyes indigestion. But, if this was a real fairy, then it might be useful. No harm in trying, anyway.

"Do you give people three wishes?" he asked.

"In your dreams, pal," said the fairy. It sat on the edge of the desk and swung legs that weren't much thicker than matchsticks. "We don't have much power these days." Then it gave a sly grin. "I can still turn milk sour. And when I snap my fingers, pencils break. Do you want me to show you?"

"No, thanks."

"Please yourself," said the fairy. "What's your name?"

"Er—it's Ross. Ross Beansack. I thought you knew all about me."

"Nope. Only that you were a writer. Okay, Ross, let's start this Save the Fairies story."

"What?" A gaping hole appeared in the big

hairy beard.

The fairy's eyes narrowed. "You heard me. You're going to write a bestseller about the little people. Start typing and I'll tell you what to say."

Chapter 2

The Little Lost People

The big hairy author scratched his beard. He didn't have much choice. It was embarrassing to share your desk with something you didn't believe in. But the sooner he got this written, the sooner the little thing would go back to Fairyland or Cartoon Town or wherever. Besides, it did have a point. No one wrote about fairies these days. You could only find real fairytales in old books that smelled of dust and mildew.

"All right. I'm ready," he said.

It wasn't easy to listen to a voice that went through his head like a screwdriver. The fairy squeaked out a sad tale about the lost little people. Fairies, elves, pixies and gnomes had all gone out of fashion and been replaced by monsters, ogres, dragons and aliens from outer space. It wasn't just. It wasn't fair. How could authors be so cruel?

Ross Beansack agreed. "It's against the Human Rights Act!"

"Don't be silly!" the little thing snarled. "Fairies aren't human. They don't have any rights. What will help us is publicity—books written about our miserable condition. So let's get on with it!"

The fairy stayed for lunch. It didn't eat anything but it sat on the edge of Ross's plate, and although Ross wasn't a fussy man, he was careful to keep his food on the other side.

"Finished?" the fairy asked.

Being a big author, Ross Beansack liked big lunches. He'd planned a second helping of chicken salad, followed by pancakes and peaches. But the fairy was in a hurry to get the story finished.

The big hairy author sighed and flicked some tomato out of his beard. He hated writing on a half-empty stomach. It was like driving across the Sahara Desert on a half-empty petrol tank. But he had a kind heart and, by now, the fairy's story had become as important to him as a story about whales or trees. So he left the table and went back to his desk, the fairy buzzing behind him like some large green dragonfly.

By mid afternoon, the story was almost finished. The fairy hovered in front of the screen. "It hasn't got a title!" it squeaked.

"I'm sorry. I can't think of one," said the big hairy author.

"It's a tale told to you by a fairy. Call it *Fairy Tale*."

Ross Beansack shrugged his shoulders. "That's not very good."

The little thing flew into such a rage that Ross feared it might bite him. "There you go again!" it shrieked. "Typical! Another horrible author!"

"No, no! I mean it's not a very clever title. I wasn't trying to—oh, all right. I'll call it *Fairy Tale*."

The fairy's wings slowed. It sat down on the desk, close to the computer. "Fine. Now print it out and send it to your publisher."

"Now?"

"Now." The fairy folded its arms. "I'll go with you to the post office."

"Stop giving me orders," said the author, growling. "I don't know your name. I don't even know if you're male or female."

"That's private information," the fairy said. "Where do you keep the envelopes?"

If the big hairy author thought that mailing the story would end the fairy's visit, he was wrong. The little thing rode in his pocket to the post office and back again to his desk. It made a bed in some bubble wrap, lay down and closed its eyes.

Ross Beansack got a bad feeling. "Don't you have somewhere to go?" he asked.

One green eye opened. "You have book launches, don't you?"

"Book launches?"

"Do you have to repeat everything I say?" The other green eye opened. "When a book's published, there's a party. We sign books. Everyone comes. It's in all the newspapers."

By now the big hairy author was seriously alarmed. "I do know what a book launch party is. But this book won't be published for at least a year."

The fairy closed its eyes again. "I can wait," it said.

Chapter 3

Losing the Plot

The very modern publisher looked over the top of her purple glasses. Her office was on the fortieth floor and she could see clear across the city. But today she was not admiring the view. She was frowning at the story in front of her. "Holly?" she called to her junior editor. "Will you find a copy of our contract with Ross Beansack?"

"Ross who?" said Holly, her high heels click-clacking to the contract cupboard.

"Beansack. Ross Beansack," said the very modern publisher. "He's the big hairy author. He's written some important books: *Save the Penguins*, *Save the Polar Bears*. He got a big award for *Save the Siberian Tiger*, and we made a heap of lovely money."

"Did we?" Holly looked hopeful.

The very modern publisher's frown deepened. "Beansack's supposed to be doing a new book about whales and the Amazon rainforest."

"Oh my!" said Holly. "I didn't know whales lived in the Amazon rainforest."

The publisher thumped her desk. "He sent a story about fairies! It's called Fairy Tale! I think he's lost the plot!"

The junior editor's heels clicked back to the publisher's desk. "That's a pity. It won't be a very good fairytale without a plot. Here's the contract you wanted."

"Just as I thought!" cried the publisher. "Whales! The rainforest! That's what he's supposed to be writing—not this trash."

Holly didn't know what to say. She was still wondering how whales moved around in the rainforest.

The publisher stabbed the story with purple fingernails. "It's nonsense, garbage, junk! Holly, I want you to send this story back to Mr. Beansack and tell him to deliver the book he promised. None of this fairy rubbish! Understand?"

"Yes. Certainly, boss. I'll do it at once."

"And when you've finished," said the very modern publisher, "get me a coffee with milk and two sugars. I've had a tiring day."

Holly took the sheets of paper and click-clacked back to her own little office. She had no large windows looking over the city, but on her desk were six red roses, a pink teddy bear and a photo of her boyfriend. She sat and started to write:

Dear Mr. Beansack,

You are a famous author, so can you tell me why whales live in the rainforest? I always thought they lived in the sea. Did they swim up the Amazon River? How do they move through the forest and what do they eat? By the way, our very modern publisher doesn't like your fairytale. She says it's lost its plot. Maybe you forgot to put that in the envelope.

Yours sincerely,
Holly Bright

Chapter 4

A Brilliant Idea

The big hairy author didn't know how to tell the fairy the bad news. The poor little thing had already planned the book launch party.

"I've got bad news," said the author. "You're going to be very disappointed."

Disappointed was not the right word. The fairy kicked and screamed and heaved paperclips across the desk. "I'll sue them! I'll put itchy powder in their pants! Beetles in their sandwiches!" It struggled to lift a large paperclip. "I'll go right up there and—and—" Grunting, it dropped the paperclip over the edge of the desk. "I'll scream in their ears like this!" Then it let out a screech so horrible that the author was sure his ears had been burned like toast. But he didn't mind too much, because the little green fairy had given him a brilliant idea.

"That's what we'll do! We'll go up there! The very modern publisher doesn't believe in fairies. She thinks I've made this up. But if she sees you, she'll change her mind." The author's beard shook with excitement. "You'll be a sensation!"

The safest place for the fairy to travel was the author's shirt pocket. He put some paper tissues in for comfort, but the train ride was long and the little thing was restless. Its arms and legs, though small, were as hard as toothpicks. Its buzzing wings tickled the author and he wanted to scratch his chest.

"Keep still!" he ordered.

"Excuse me?" said the woman next to him.

"Sorry, I didn't mean you," the author said.

"Then who did you mean?"

He felt he had to explain. "I'm a published children's writer. When I'm making up a story, I sometimes talk out loud."

The woman didn't believe him. She sniffed and moved to another seat.

The author pulled open his shirt pocket and whispered into it. "We'll be in the city in ten minutes. The very modern publisher's office is near the train station. Just relax."

"I can't!" The scratchy voice was as small as a pin. "This is very traumatic. Fairies never go near cities."

"What?" The author remembered to talk softly. "This was your idea, remember."

"It wasn't."

"Yes, it was. You said you were going to—"

The fairy hit him with a small but very sharp elbow. "There's a difference between saying and doing. You're a writer. You should know that."

The author patted his pocket gently with a fat finger. "Don't worry," he said. "I'll look after you."

Chapter 5

Squeals and Sour Milk

The rest of the journey went well. From the station to the tall building and all the way up in the lift, the fairy sat still. But when the big hairy author got out at the fortieth floor, something happened. Holly Bright, the junior editor, dropped a pile of stories on the floor outside the office.

The author hurried to help her pick them up. As he bent over, two crumpled tissues fell out of his shirt pocket and something else took off in a flash of green.

"Oh my!" cried Holly. "A big green moth! My boss hates moths! She'll go bananas!"

The author saw the green thing whiz through the publisher's doorway and almost immediately he heard the scream. By the time he got into the office, the very modern publisher was standing on her desk, yelling loudly and flapping her hands. Her purple glasses were on the floor, broken, and her chair was lying with its legs in the air. The fairy was racing around the room in a blur of green light.

"Moth! Moth!" shrieked the publisher. "Holly! Get the insect spray."

The big hairy author tried to explain but his voice got buried under the noise. All he could do was grab the can of insect spray from Holly and throw it down the hallway as far as he could.

The publisher could not see well without her glasses. She pointed with a moving finger and screamed. "Hit it! Whack it! Squash it with a book!"

That was too much for the fairy. It started the terrible squealing noise and both Holly and the publisher clapped their hands over their ears. The big hairy author put two fingers in his mouth and whistled. Then he pulled open the top of his shirt pocket. The flash of green sped across the room and dropped inside. It was trembling. The author could feel the fast ticking of its heart. The poor little thing was utterly terrified.

"Find that moth!" the publisher screamed at Holly. "Kill it! Squash it flat!"

The big hairy author tiptoed out of the office and down the hallway. As he waited for the lift, he said to the fairy, "I've got a better idea. I'll publish your story myself. We'll still have a launch party. You can help me sign books. All the newspaper and TV reporters will be there. That's a promise."

Back in the office, the very modern publisher was ordering Holly to call the pest control people. "They'll find the moth!" she said. "They'll spray the office from top to bottom. It can't get away."

Holly looked for a pencil to write down the number of the pest control company, but every pencil she picked up had a broken point. "Oh my!" she said. "There isn't a decent pencil in the entire place!"

The very modern publisher turned her chair the right way up. She sat down and fanned herself with someone's story. "I need a cup of coffee, Holly. Milk and two sugars. And hurry!"

Ten minutes later, Holly returned with black coffee. "Sorry, boss. All the milk is sour."

"Then go out and get fresh milk!" snapped the publisher.

"I did," said Holly. "But the moment I walked into the office, the milk went yucky and solid with blue stuff growing on it. It must be something to do with global warming." Then she smiled. "Why don't you get Mr. Beansack to write a book called *Save the Weather*?"

From the Author

I might be messy and greedy but I'm not as extreme as the big hairy author, and I'm glad to say that all my publishers are very nice. However, I'm aware that there are fads and fashions in books. These days certain stories are definitely unfashionable and publishers are likely to say, "No thanks" to the author who writes them.

For years, books about fairies and magic have been unpopular with the adult world. So what happens when a small angry fairy visits the big hairy author and insists that he write about neglected little people? Can you guess what the very modern publisher says when she's expecting a story about saving whales and instead gets a fairy story?

Her words do not make polite reading!

Joy Cowley

From the Illustrator

A big hairy author, a shrieking fairy, a rubbish dump and ghosts, what more could an illustrator ask for?

I had a lot of fun drawing the characters for this series. Each one had their own personality which I wanted to show in the way they looked.

As I read the stories I started to picture the scenes in my head. I could see the publisher in her modern purple suit up on her desk screaming, while the little green fairy flies madly around the room. I laughed as I imagined the roly poly Ross Beansack rolling around among the smelly rubbish inside the dumpster, or huddled up in the dark, munching away on a cookie, waiting for ghosts.

I'm not as big and hairy as Ross Beansack, but looking around my messy studio while I chew on a snack, I realize I might share some of his bad habits.

Ian Forss